HOPSCOTCH ADVENTURES

Arthur the King

Tales

Ess

First published in 2006 by
Franklin Watts
338 Euston Road
London
NW1 3BH

Franklin Watts Australia
Level 17/207 Kent Street
Sydney
NSW 2000

Text © Karen Wallace 2006
Illustration © Neil Chapman 2006

A CIP catalogue record for this book is available
from the British Library.

ISBN 978 0 7496 6695 8

Series Editor: Jackie Hamley
Series Advisor: Dr Barrie Wade
Series Designer: Peter Scoulding

Printed in China

Franklin Watts is a division of
Hachette Children's Books,
an Hachette UK company.
www.hachette.co.uk

Arthur
the King

by Karen Wallace and Neil Chapman

W
FRANKLIN WATTS
LONDON·SYDNEY

Arthur was King of Britain, but he still had to fight for his kingdom.

His worst enemy was Lord Pellinor.
"I shall defeat this traitor,"
cried Arthur.

He grabbed a spear and
rode into the forest.

"You are not as strong as Lord Pellinor," warned Merlin the magician. "Turn back!" But Arthur didn't listen.

Arthur charged at Lord Pellinor,
but he broke his own spear.
So he fought with his sword.

Lord Pellinor smashed
Arthur's sword to pieces.
"I will kill you now!" he cried.

Merlin appeared. "If you kill King Arthur, you will destroy Britain," he said.

"King Arthur is a brave knight," said Lord Pellinor. "If he agrees, I will serve him instead."

Arthur was so badly hurt that he heard nothing.

When Arthur woke up, he was safe with Merlin. The magician gave him medicine and healed all his wounds.

"Come with me," said Merlin.
"A king needs a sword." They
rode to the magic land of Avalon.

They stopped at a lake and
stepped into a boat. It floated
into the middle of the water.

Suddenly, the lake turned silver around them. Then an arm appeared with a sword in its hand.

Arthur was amazed.

"Is that for me?" he asked.

"Yes," replied Merlin.

"The sword is called Excalibur."

The boat took them back to their
horses. "We will meet Lord
Pellinor in the forest," warned
Merlin. "Let him pass."
"This time I will kill him
with Excalibur," cried Arthur.

"No," said Merlin. "He will serve
you well and his sons will become
your bravest knights.

"Arthur, you must learn how to
become a wise king!" Arthur looked
longingly at Excalibur and sighed.

"Which do you like better?" asked Merlin. "The sword or this shield?"
"The sword," cried Arthur.

"You are unwise," said Merlin.
"The shield will protect you from
wounds. Carry it always."

At that moment, Lord Pellinor rode past. Merlin wove a spell so he could not see them. Arthur wanted to fight but he stayed where he was.

"Well done," said Merlin.
"Remember, things are not
always as they appear."

When they arrived at his castle, Arthur showed everyone Excalibur. "You are the bravest knight in the land," cried his knights. "Now, with that sword, you are the most powerful, too!"

With Merlin's help, Arthur grew up to be a wise and powerful king.

And, in time, Lord Pellinor and his sons became some of Arthur's bravest, most loyal knights.

Hopscotch has been specially designed to fit the requirements of the Literacy Framework. It offers real books by top authors and illustrators for children developing their reading skills. There are lots of Hopscotch stories to choose from:

Find out more about all the Hopscotch books at:
www.franklinwatts.co.uk

* **hardback**